WITH SPECIAL THANKS TO LINDA CHAPMAN

First published in Great Britain in 2012 by Simon and Schuster UK Ltd
A CBS COMPANY

Text Copyright © Hothouse Fiction Limited 2012
Illustrations copyright © Mary Hall 2012
Designed by Amy Cooper

3 5 7 9 10 8 6 4 2

Simon & Schuster UK Ltd
1st Floor, 222 Gray's Inn Road
London
WC1X 8HB

Simon & Schuster Australia, Sydney

Simon & Schuster India, New Delhi

A CIP catalogue record for this book is available from the British Library.

ISBN 978-0-85707-881-0

Printed and bound in Great Britain by CPI Group (UK) Ltd, Croydon, CR0 4YY

www.simonandschuster.co.uk
www.simonandschuster.com.au
www.spellsisters.co.uk

AMBER CASTLE

# AMELIA
## THE SILVER SISTER

Illustrations by Mary Hall

SIMON & SCHUSTER

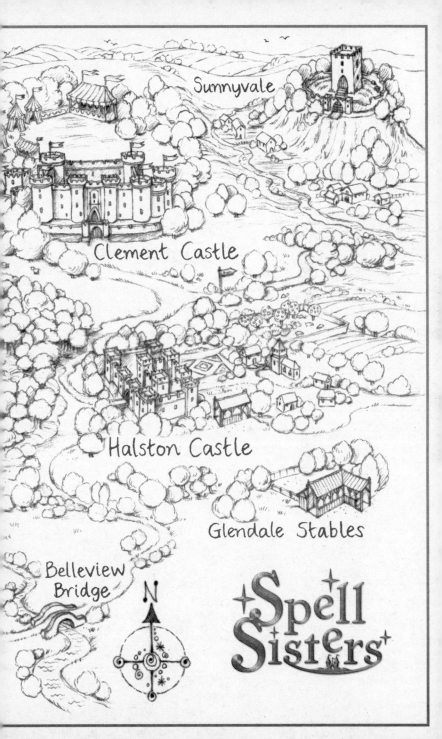

Sunnyvale

Clement Castle

Halston Castle

Glendale Stables

Belleview
Bridge

N

Spell
Sisters

# On a Wooded Hill

The old round castle nestled on a hilltop. A crumbling outer wall and a moat surrounded it, with a wooden drawbridge across the muddy water. A round tower stood in the centre, with a wooden staircase leading up to a large oak door.

The door swung open and a beautiful woman with hair as black as a bat's wing marched out.

A raven was perched on her shoulder, and in her hands she held a silver crown. Striding down the staircase, she stopped in the grassy keep, the early morning breeze whispering through her hair.

'See what I can do, my beauty!' Morgana hissed to her raven. She waved her right hand above the points of the crown. Instantly, the rubies and emeralds changed to dark jet stones, and the silver of the crown began to grow dull. Morgana's lips curved into a delighted smile. She clicked her fingers and watched as the metal slowly bent into twisted shapes.

'Behold!' she said, holding the crown up to the raven. 'With the magic I have stolen from my sister Amelia, I can now make minerals and metals appear and disappear, and move them to my will.' She laughed triumphantly. 'And what's more, soon the island of Avalon will be mine at last!'

The raven cawed and put his head on one side as if asking a question.

'Those girls?' Morgana snarled. 'No, they shall not stop me.'

Pulling a small dark crystal ball from her pocket, she muttered a word. An image flickered inside the glass, showing a tall girl with deep red hair and a shorter, very pretty, blonde girl. They were in a bedchamber, chatting and laughing as they packed clothes into travelling trunks. Morgana's eyes narrowed.

'Look at them! They are nothing but children. They may have rescued three of my sisters, but all *eight* must be freed by the time of the next lunar eclipse if they are to stop me taking Avalon for my own. Time is running out for them

– the eclipse is approaching soon. They will not defeat me!'

The raven cawed in delight. Thrusting the ball back in her pocket, Morgana lifted the crown. Placing it on her head, she smiled. . .

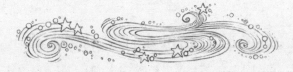

# Getting Ready to Go

Gwen watched as her cousin Flora carefully smoothed the creases out of her mother's new red dress as it lay in the travelling case and smiled. Flora pushed her long blonde plaits behind her shoulders with a flourish. 'Oh, I'm so excited!' she declared. 'I can't *wait* to go to this tournament. Just think of all the beautiful ladies and handsome knights we're going to see.'

Her blue eyes grew dreamy. 'And there'll be dancing, music and feasting in the evenings, and I can wear my new blue dress! It'll be so much fun!'

'I can't wait either – but I just want to see all the horses and watch the competitions!' Gwen said with a laugh, packing her aunt's headdresses and cloaks into another trunk. Gwen loved tournaments, where knights would take part in lots of different contests over three or four days. There was jousting, where the knights had to charge at each other on horseback and try and knock each other off using a long stick called a lance, and sword fighting. . . Gwen smiled again just thinking about it. It was all so exciting! At the end of the tournament, one knight was announced the winner.

Sometimes the tournaments were held far away and then Gwen's uncle, Sir Richard, would go off on his own to compete with his squire and pages. This time, though, the tournament was being held at Clement Castle, which was not that far, so Gwen's Aunt Matilda, Flora's mother, had said that the entire household could go and watch. And as the events would be going on for a few days, arrangements had been made for everyone to stay at the castle. Gwen and Flora had been looking forward to it for days.

Gwen sighed happily as she shut the travelling case, her tangle of shoulder-length dark red hair bouncing with her excitement. 'This one's going to be even more fun because there's going to be a contest for the squires and pages this afternoon before the main fighting starts tomorrow. I can't wait to see it!'

Flora gave her a teasing look. 'I'm surprised you're not planning on disguising yourself as a boy and entering yourself!'

'I wish I could!' Gwen said yearningly. She loved doing all the things the pages did. But although she was allowed to ride and use a bow and arrow near the manor grounds, tournaments were strictly forbidden for her, or any girls.

Flora's blue eyes widened. 'Imagine how cross Mother would be if you did enter!'

'I know.' Gwen really *had* considered disguising herself, but pages didn't wear proper armour when they fought in contests and she knew her aunt would be bound to spot her. 'If Aunt Matilda found out, she'd ban me from going outside, and that would be very bad news.' Gwen's hand reached for the large blue pendant that hung on a silver chain around her neck. It glittered like the sea in sunlight.

Flora nodded. The two girls shared a secret.

They had found
the blue pendant
trapped in a rock
by the Lake in
the nearby woods
one day while they
were exploring and
when Gwen had pulled it free, a beautiful lady
had risen up through the waters. Her name was
Nineve, the Lady of the Lake, and she had told
them that it was written in the stars that whoever
who pulled the pendant from the rock would be
able to help save the kingdom.

Nineve had gone on to explain that the
magical island of Avalon in the centre of the
Lake was dying because the eight Spell Sisters
who lived there had been imprisoned by their
elder sister, the evil sorceress Morgana Le Fay.

All of the sisters had to be returned to the island by the time of the next lunar eclipse, or Morgana would be able to take control of Avalon and bring devastation to the kingdom.

Gwen and Flora had agreed to help and so far Nineve's magic had tracked down three of the sisters and the girls had rescued them safely.

'I wonder when Nineve will contact us again,' said Flora softly.

'At least Clement Castle is not too far from the Lake', Gwen said. 'If Nineve sends us a message we can easily get to her. The eclipse must be drawing near, so we're running out of time. We have to free the remaining sisters and stop Morgana!' Her brow knitted with concern.

'Yes, we must! Let's just hope Nineve finds the next sister soon,' Flora said, nodding. She spun round to fetch some herbs from the table to place in the travelling cases and keep the dresses smelling nice, but as she did so, she lost her footing, tripping over a pair of shoes left on the floor – Gwen had to reach out quickly and grab her cousin's arm to stop her from falling.

'Be careful!' Gwen chuckled.

Flora tutted. 'If there was a contest for the clumsiest person at this tournament, I'd be bound to win it!'

Just then the door opened and Aunt Matilda swept in. 'Well, girls, are all my things packed?'

'Yes, Mother!' said Flora quickly, adding a sprig of thyme to the top of the clothing.

Gwen shut the bolts of the case she had been packing. 'This trunk is packed too, Aunt Matilda.'

'Well done, Guinevere – and you too, Flora,' said Aunt Matilda. She went to the looking glass and checked her reflection, smoothing down a few stray strands of fair hair. 'Now go and tidy yourselves up and put on your travelling things. I shall see you outside shortly.'

Gwen and Flora looked at one another excitedly. It was almost time to go!

# 2

# Off to Clement Castle!

The manor household gathered in the grassy area enclosed by the outer stone walls. Gwen had come to live at her aunt and uncle's large manor a few years ago, just like a lot of girls and boys were sent to live with relatives when they were about eight or nine. The girls would help dress the ladies of the house and learn skills like singing and needlework. The boys would start as pages, acquiring the skills they would one day need when they became knights. Gwen and Flora were the only young girls in Sir Richard's castle, but there were eight pages.

Gwen and Flora had already mounted their ponies and were waiting to set off. Both girls were wearing their thick wool travelling cloaks and leather outdoor boots. The keep was filled with the sounds of shouting and horses snorting and stamping as the servants loaded up the cart with the last few parcels of food and the final bits of luggage. Sir Richard was in full armour, seated on his majestic grey stallion, Valiant, who was striking out and squealing when other horses came too close.

Aunt Matilda was not fond of riding or walking, so she was going to travel inside a carriage decorated in blue and silver silks, carried by two horses – one in front and one behind.

Gwen's pony, Merrylegs, pawed at the ground, just as eager as she was to be off. He was one of the liveliest ponies in the stables and Gwen loved him almost as much as the magical stallion, Moonlight, that the girls had ridden on their magical adventures to save the Spell Sisters.

'Steady, boy,' Gwen said, leaning forward to stroke her pony's warm, grey neck. Just at that moment, another pony barged into her. Gwen felt Merrylegs jump to one side and it was only by clinging on like a cat that she managed to stay in the saddle. Luckily, she was a very good rider and within seconds, Gwen had her pony under control. She looked round, irritated, to see who was responsible.

Will, the oldest and tallest of the pages, who liked to pick on anyone younger than him, was

grinning at her mockingly from the back of a dappled pony, Basil. 'Having trouble controlling your pony, Gwen?'

'No,' Gwen said. 'I think you're the one who's having trouble.'

'I think you should find a different pony,' Will called as Merrylegs sidestepped. 'He's far too lively for a *girl* to handle.'

'He's only upset because *you* rode into him!' Gwen said, glaring at Will.

He raised his bushy eyebrows. 'Rode into him? I don't know what you're talking about! I didn't do anything.' He laughed slyly. 'If you can't control your pony, maybe you should ask Arthur to lead you to the castle. I bet he'd be happy to!' Will made kissing noises.

'I'm sure he would – he's a *real* gentleman!' Gwen retorted. Arthur was Gwen's friend and another page at the manor, and Gwen was sure Will was jealous of him. He was already doing very well, and she was certain Arthur would make a great knight one day.

Just then, Arthur came riding up beside them, but he reined his pony in just a fraction too late. Basil moved back a little bit in alarm, and Will lost his balance. Gwen saw Arthur give Basil a quick, sharp slap on the rump, and Will lost his grip altogether, bumping down on to the ground as his pony trotted away.

'Whoops! Sorry, Will,' said Arthur, looking

surprised. 'You seem to have fallen off!' He held out his hand to help the older boy up.

'I didn't just fall off! You jolted my pony!'

Will exclaimed, his face crimson as he ignored Arthur's hand and scrambled to his feet, his travelling cloak now muddy.

Arthur turned to Gwen, raising his eyebrows innocently. 'I don't know what he's talking about!'

He and Gwen grinned at each other as Will

cursed under his breath and set off after Basil. The pony had trotted to the other side of the keep and was munching on apples on the cart, ignoring the cook who was shouting at him.

'Thanks,' Gwen said.

'I saw what he did,' said Arthur. 'Will's getting too big for his boots. I hope someone teaches him a lesson in the pages' contest today.'

'Maybe it will be you,' said Gwen.

'Maybe,' Arthur replied with a grin. Then he leaned forward and spoke in a low voice. 'I've packed your bow and quiver.'

'Oh, thanks, Arthur!' Gwen whispered with a smile she had given them to Arthur to take to the tournament as she wanted to have them there just in case Nineve called her and Flora to come to the Lake while they were away. Gwen knew her aunt wouldn't have approved of her taking her bow and arrow, so she had asked Arthur to pack them with his things. Of course, she had to keep the real reason a secret.

'I'll leave them with the other bows in the tent and you can pick them up from there when you want them,' Arthur said. 'Are you planning on going out into the forest around Castle Clement then?'

'Uh, perhaps,' Gwen answered vaguely. 'I thought it'd be good to have them, in case I do.'

All the other pages started gathering behind Sir Richard. 'It looks like we're about to go,' Arthur said. 'See you later!'

Gwen called a goodbye and watched him trot off. Flora rode up beside her. Her blue eyes were glinting teasingly. 'So, what was Arthur talking to you about? Did he ask you for your favour?'

'Of course not!' Gwen protested. Before

knights competed in a tournament, they would often approach a lady they thought was very beautiful and ask for something called her 'favour'. She would give them a glove, or a ribbon, and the knight would attach it to his horse or armour, like a lucky charm.

'Are you sure?' Flora pressed, grinning.

'Yes! You know it's nothing like that between Arthur and me. We're just friends.'

'OK,' Flora said, and then sighed. 'Oh, it would be so nice to be asked to give someone your favour! Maybe one of the squires or pages will ask me.' She held up her wrist to show Gwen a blue ribbon she had wrapped round it, and smiled. 'I've got this just in case!'

Gwen shook her head and chuckled. She and Flora could not be more different. It hadn't even occurred to her that a squire or page might ask for a favour!

There was a loud shout, and they looked round to see Sir Richard brandishing his sword in the air. It caught the rays of the pale autumn sun and then Sir Richard sent Valiant galloping out across the drawbridge and down the hill into the autumn woods. The group of pages called out too, and charged out behind him. Gwen felt a surge of longing – oh, if only she could do that too! But she and Flora had to ride slowly beside her aunt's carriage with the servants and packhorses following behind. How dull! Still, soon enough, to the sound of snorts and hoof beats, shouts and cartwheels rumbling, she and the rest of the household set off.

# Fortunes and Magic

lement Castle was an imposing grey building owned by Sir William, an old knight who no longer competed at tournaments himself, but still loved to watch them. The tournament would take place on the meadows beneath the castle.

As they arrived, Gwen saw that the lists – the area where the fighting would take place

– had been roped off, and a wooden grandstand had been put up for the noble folk to watch from. Brightly coloured silk banners fluttered in the breeze. Around the edge of the lists there were lots of pavilions – small brightly coloured tents that had been set up for the knights who would be taking part. The whole area was bustling with people: villagers crowded the meadows, pages were leading horses around, while the knights strode about in their armour and ladies in beautiful dresses chatted to each other. It was all so exciting!

As soon as they had unpacked everything, Gwen and Flora put on their new dresses and cloaks and went downstairs. The noise and bustle on the ground floor of the castle was incredible as servants hurried about preparing the food for the first night's feast. Gwen breathed in the smell of game pie and roast hog and could feel her tummy rumbling! However, it was a long while until supper. First there were the pages' and squires' contests to watch.

The girls hurried outside, across the drawbridge and down the hill to the meadow. 'Look at all the silks. Aren't they beautiful?' said Flora as they made their way down the slope. She was so busy looking around that she didn't see where she was going, and walked straight into someone.

'Oh! I beg your pardon!' she gasped, her

cheeks turning scarlet as she jumped back.

The handsome, brown-haired boy she had knocked into bowed low and then shook his head. 'That is quite all right,' he said politely. 'It is my pleasure to have met such a beautiful young lady.' He smiled and continued on his way.

Flora's cheeks turned even redder. 'Oh!' she said, blushing in delight.

Gwen giggled at Flora's expression. 'See, sometimes it's not so bad being clumsy, is it? Come on. Let's go to the pavilions.'

Linking arms, they hurried on through the crowd. A peddler had set up a stall selling bits of cloth, ribbons, mittens, hats, scarves and buttons. 'Can we have a look?' Flora asked eagerly.

'Do we have to?' groaned Gwen. She knew Flora could look at buttons and ribbons for ages.

'Yes!' said Flora with a laugh, running to the

stall. The peddler had his back to her as he sorted through some items on display. He was wearing a long dark green cloak and had very long white hair that fell halfway down his back. Gwen waited a little way off. Standing near to her was a knot of local villagers who were nodding in the peddler's direction and talking in low voices. Curious as to what they were saying, Gwen moved closer.

'He's supposed to be able to do magic,' she heard a large woman whispering. 'He visited my cousin's village, and she said she saw him vanish before her very eyes!'

'Probably with half the lord's silver!' snorted another.

'No. It's true; he's *magic* they say,' the first one insisted. There was an intake of breath from the whole group.

'Never!'

'Not really!'

The first woman nodded and folded her arms. 'He conjured a white bird from nowhere. And he can tell fortunes too.'

The villagers all stared at the stallholder. Gwen's forehead crinkled. It couldn't be true, could it? But then again, she knew magic was real. She'd seen it with her own eyes with the

Spell Sisters and Nineve!

Flora was now picking up some rainbow-coloured buttons and looking at them closely. Gwen went to join her.

The old man behind the stall suddenly turned around as Gwen walked over. He had a very old, lined face, but the brightest blue eyes she had ever seen. 'Come to buy some pretty buttons, my dear?' he asked, looking at Flora.

'Maybe,' she smiled at him. 'They're very beautiful.'

'And what about you, child? Maybe some ribbons, a new brooch. . .?' As he spoke, Gwen saw his gaze fall on her pendant. His eyes instantly flicked to hers, and she had the strangest feeling that the old man was looking deep into her mind.

'Well, well, well,' he said. 'So it is you.'

Flora looked surprised. She glanced at Gwen.

The old man leaned closer. 'Shall I tell your fortune, child?'

Flora put her arm through Gwen's protectively. 'Maybe we should go.' She tugged at her, but Gwen shook her head. There was something about the old man that in a strange way reminded her of Nineve. Maybe it was the sparkle in his eyes? Or the feeling of calm that seemed to come from him?

Gwen hesitated and then boldly held out her hand. 'Yes, all right. Tell my fortune.'

Flora caught her breath. 'Gwen! I really don't think this is a good idea.'

But Gwen ignored her. The old man nodded, then put his hands around hers and stared for a long moment at her palm.

Gwen swallowed. It felt as if her heart had stopped beating. He looked up. 'There is much to come for you, my dear, but it is not my place to speak of it all now,' he said, talking so softly she had to lean close to him to hear. 'This, however, I can tell you.' He took a breath, and then spoke in a sing-song voice:

'To a nearby castle you will go
And there confront your greatest foe
In a valley named for light
An evil darkness to put right.'

One thought flashed through Gwen's mind. Her quest to free the Spell Sisters of Avalon!

'Is it to do with—?' she began.

'Shh!' the old man interrupted. 'Do not speak your thoughts aloud. There are too many curious

ears.' He glanced towards the group of villagers and leaned forward again. 'What I have told you will come in useful soon,' he murmured. 'Remember it.'

'I will.' Gwen turned and walked over to where Flora had backed off a few paces. Suddenly she thought of something and ran back to the old man.

'What's your name?' she asked.

A mysterious smile pulled at his lips. 'I have many names, but Merlin is the one I go by in this time and place. Remember it well, Guinevere. Our paths shall cross again one day. In the mean time, may the magic of Avalon help you on your current quest.'

Gwen stared. How did he know her name?

And what did he know about Avalon and what she was trying to do? She opened her mouth to ask him, but she was too late. He had already turned away to talk to a new customer. Gwen walked back to Flora, her head spinning.

'What a strange old man,' said Flora with a shiver.

'Very strange,' Gwen breathed. 'I think he's magic. He knew my name, and he seemed to know about Avalon too. He told my fortune, or part of it at least. It was sort of like a poem.' She repeated the rhyme to Flora, who stared at her with wide eyes.

'That sounds frightening,' Flora said. '*Evil darkness*? Greatest foe? It has to mean Morgana, doesn't it?'

Gwen nodded. 'I wish I could talk to him some more.'

'Gwen?' Flora looked as though a horrible thought had just crossed her mind. 'What if he's working for Morgana in secret or something? She could be trying to trick us.'

Gwen shook her head. 'No,' she said softly. 'He's good. I know he is. He's just like Nineve and the Spell Sisters. His words are going to help us. I can feel it.' She put her arm through Flora's again. 'I just hope we hear from Nineve soon.'

'Me too,' said Flora.

Gwen smiled. 'Anyway, come on. Until we do hear from her, can we go to the pavilions?'

Flora nodded and laughed. Giving Merlin one last look, Gwen walked away arm in arm with her friend.

# A New Adventure

Gwen and Flora found the pages milling about next to Sir Richard's blue and silver pavilion. All of the boys had changed into their smartest tunics, cloaks and breeches. Some of them were even wearing hats, and Gwen noticed that Will's was typically over the top. It was white with an enormous blue feather on it, and he kept touching it proudly.

Some of the pages were wrestling; others were comparing bows and arrows, while the rest stood around laughing and talking. A small blond boy who looked about six years old was playing with Arthur, trying to wrestle the older boy to the ground.

'You got me, Mark!' Arthur cried, pretending that the boy had managed to pin him to the ground. 'I am defeated!'

He fell over and the little boy put one foot on his chest. 'I won! I won!'

'Why don't you go and play somewhere else?' muttered Will. 'We've got more important things to do.'

The little boy pulled a cheeky face at him. 'Why have you got a dead bird on your head?'

Will's face darkened. 'Why you. . .'

Arthur jumped quickly to his feet. 'Come

on, Mark. You can have a piggyback ride with Luke!' He hastily lifted the boy up on to one of the other page's shoulders. Mark hooted with laughter and kicked Luke on.

'Who is he?' Gwen asked, going over to Arthur.

'Mark D'Gancy. He's the nephew of Sir William who owns the castle here. We've been asked to keep an eye on him during the tournament.'

'It's really annoying!' said Will, looking disgruntled. 'We're supposed to be knights in training, not nursemaids. I think we should just be mean to him, then he'll run back to his mother and we'll be free of him.'

'Oh, come on, Will,' said Arthur. 'It's only while the tournament is on. Don't you remember being that young and wanting to be with the older pages?'

Will just snorted in reply.

'I must say, that's an *interesting* hat, Will,' Gwen said, biting back a chuckle as she caught Flora's eye.

'Very *interesting*!' Flora giggled.

'It's the latest fashion,' Will said, stroking the feather vainly.

Gwen didn't dare look at Flora because she knew she'd explode with laughter. Will looked ridiculous!

Just then, Luke came jogging towards them, with Mark still on his back. 'Charge!' the little boy shouted, riding Luke straight towards Will. Mark jabbed Will with a twig he had picked up, pretending it was a lance.

'Ow!' yelled Will.

Mark giggled mischievously and jumped

down from Luke's back. Will stepped towards him angrily, but Arthur quickly put himself between them.

'What do you think you're doing? Get out of my way!' Will growled.

Arthur shook his head. 'Remember, Will, it's a knight's duty to protect the weak.'

Will met his gaze for a moment, but then gave up. 'Gah!' He stomped off, the blue feather wobbling in his hat.

'Well said, cousin Arthur!' called a boy with dark brown hair who was standing nearby, watching.

'Gawain!' cried Arthur, going over to greet him.

Gawain was tall and broad-shouldered, with fun-filled green eyes and a wide smile. Gwen recognised him as the boy Flora had bumped into earlier.

'It's good to see you!' he said, clasping hands with Arthur. 'How have you been keeping, Arthur?'

'Very well, thank you!'

Gwen went forward curiously. 'Hello!'

'This is Gwen. She lives at Halston Castle too, and she can shoot better than any of the pages!' said Arthur with an admiring smile. 'Don't ever take her on in an archery contest, Gawain.'

'I won't,' laughed Gawain. 'Pleased to meet you, Gwen.' His gaze fell on Flora. Gwen saw a new warmth coming into his eyes. 'And this is. . .?' he said.

'Flora, my cousin,' said Gwen quickly.

Gawain reached for Flora's hand. 'What a beautiful name. It is a great pleasure to meet you properly, Flora.' He kissed her hand politely.

Flora blushed deeply. 'And . . . and you,' she stammered shyly. 'Are you in the contest?'

'Of course!' Gawain declared.

Gwen noticed Flora playing with the ribbon around her wrist again and saw Gawain glance at it too. She cleared her throat dramatically.

'Arthur, come over here a second. I need to talk to you!' She pulled him away.

'What is it?' he asked.

'Nothing,' she whispered, her eyes on Flora and Gawain. Now the two of them were alone, she saw Flora laugh and nod, then untie the ribbon from her wrist. He must have asked for Flora's favour! 'Look!' she hissed to Arthur. She clasped her hands together happily, knowing how pleased Flora would be.

'Gwen. . .' Arthur said suddenly 'Would you . . . I mean. . . well. . .'

'Come on!' Gwen darted back across the grass to Flora's side, just as Gawain bowed.

'We'd better go and get ready for the contest,' he said.

'I'll be watching!' promised Flora, her eyes shining.

Gawain nodded. 'Come on, Arthur.'

'Well, I was just going to. . . to. . .' Arthur looked at Gwen, then hesitated. 'Oh, it doesn't matter,' he said, his cheeks turning slightly red. 'I'll see you afterwards, Gwen.'

Gwen nodded. 'Good luck! I'll be cheering you on!' Their eyes met and Arthur smiled broadly.

✦ ✦ ✦

The trumpets sounded and everyone gathered around. Flora and Gwen took their seats in the stand with the other noble folk. First of all, the pages paraded round on their ponies. Unlike the knights, they did not fight wearing armour, and they used short blunt swords and lances. Gwen watched anxiously as the competition started. How would Arthur do?

She needn't have worried. Although he was not as big as some of the older pages, Arthur was very strong and agile. He managed to wrestle Will to the ground and beat him in the sword fight easily, much to Will's irritation. Soon there was just Arthur and Gawain left in the competition. Gawain was taller and stronger, and an excellent fighter, but Arthur was very determined and the two cousins refused to give each other an inch. Back and forth they went, up and down the meadow, until they were both soaked with sweat.

*Come on, Arthur!* thought Gwen, crossing her fingers.

Beside her she could hear Flora whisper, 'Come on, Gawain!'

Suddenly Gwen felt a familiar tingling feeling. She looked down and saw that her blue pendant was sparkling with a silvery light! She hastily put her hand over it and glanced around, checking no one had noticed. 'Flora! Nineve's sending us a message! Let's go and find somewhere quiet,' she whispered.

Luckily, everyone was so busy watching the competition that they didn't notice the two girls slipping away. They found a quiet spot in the shadow of the castle walls. Gwen took the pendant off and held it in her hands. 'Nineve! We're here!'

A mist seemed to swirl through the centre of the shining pendant. As it cleared, the girls saw Nineve's beautiful face, encircled by her long chestnut hair, looking out at them.

'Guinevere. Flora!' Her voice was soft and musical. 'I have found another of the Spell Sisters of Avalon.'

'Oh, thank goodness!' said Gwen.

'She is called Amelia,' Nineve continued. 'She's the sister who has power over minerals and metals.'

Gwen and Flora exchanged excited looks.

It was time for another adventure! 'We'll come to the Lake,' Gwen whispered eagerly.

'Wonderful, girls. When you arrive, I shall use my magic to show you all I know about where Amelia is trapped.'

'Let's go now,' Flora said. 'As soon as

Gawain and Arthur have finished fighting, the squires will start their contest, and that will go on for the rest of the afternoon. No one will notice we've gone as long as we're back for the feast at sunset.'

Gwen nodded. 'We'll come straight away,' she promised Nineve.

Nineve smiled. 'Thank you!'

The mist swirled over the pendant again, and when it cleared, Nineve had gone. Gwen slipped the pendant back over her head; it clinked next to the three beautiful gems that also hung from the chain. The three Spell Sisters whom she and Flora had rescued so far had each given her a gem as a gift to say thank you. There was a fire agate stone from Sophia, an emerald from Lily and an amber piece from Isabella. Perhaps she would get another gem that day. For a moment,

Gwen remembered what Merlin had said to her:

*'To a nearby castle you will go*
*And there confront your greatest foe. . .'*

Morgana was bound to try and stop them. Gwen took a deep breath. Whatever Morgana tried, they would fight her. They were going to rescue Amelia, and nothing was going to stand in their way!

# 5

## To the Lake!

Gwen and Flora hurried away from the castle. Behind them there was the sound of cheering and applause. One of the pages must have won. Gwen couldn't help wondering who it was, but she pushed the thought to the back of her mind. Right now there were far more important things to think about.

'Before we go, I want to fetch my bow and

arrows,' she told Flora. 'Can we go to Uncle Richard's pavilion and get them? Arthur said he would leave them there.'

They rushed over to the blue and silver pavilion. Gwen was about to slip inside and try to find her bow and arrows among the other weapons when she heard the sound of laughing and shouting coming towards the tent. She glanced round. Some of the pages were now walking back towards the pavilion. There was no sign of Arthur or Gawain, but Will was there still wearing his silly hat. With him were Tom, Edmund and Luke. Little Mark was at the front. 'Arthur won! Arthur won!' he shouted, dancing around.

Gwen felt her heart leap.

Luke smiled. 'That's enough now, Mark. Remember, no true knight ever crows about a victory, particularly not after a fight that was so evenly matched.'

'But he still won!' whooped Mark.

'Oh, get out of the way, little squirt,' said Will, pushing him to one side. Mark stumbled and fell over in the mud.

'Will, don't treat him like that!' Luke protested.

'Why not? He's as annoying as a bluebottle!' said Will.

Mark glared at him, but didn't dare say anything as he got to his feet. He stomped away. Gwen wanted to check he was all right, but she was also desperate to get her bow and arrows so she and Flora could head to the Lake. How were they going to get away without the boys seeing them?

Just then, Flora pointed. 'Look,' she said. Gwen saw Arthur being carried over on the shoulders of some of the other pages. Gawain was with him.

'You won!' Gwen cried, racing over in spite of herself.

Arthur grinned. 'I did. But only just.' He jumped down from the other pages' shoulders. 'You almost had me, cousin,' he said to Gawain.

'It was a stroke of luck that gave me the fight in the end.'

Gawain's handsome face broke into a good-natured grin. 'You were the worthy winner today, Arthur. Well done!' He saw Flora and went over to her.

'Your favour brought me luck. Coming second to Arthur is no shame. Thank you.' Flora blushed.

While everyone was still chatting, Gwen pulled Arthur to one side. 'Do you think you could find my bow and quiver?' she whispered.

'Now?' Arthur said in surprise.

She nodded. 'Flora and I want to go and explore the forest before supper.'

He smiled. 'All right, I'll get them for you.'

Arthur went into the pavilion. Gwen waited and waited, growing more anxious with each minute. Nineve would be expecting them, and they needed to go and free Amelia. Flora glanced over at her questioningly, and Gwen shrugged helplessly.

At last, Arthur came out, looking puzzled. 'I don't know where they are,' he told Gwen. 'I'm sorry. I'm sure I left them here, but they've gone. I'll have a look again later. Anyway, if you go into the forest now, won't you miss the squires' contest?'

Gwen hesitated, torn. She didn't want to go without her bow and arrows, but she and Flora had to get to the Lake as soon as possible.

'You go ahead. I think Flora and I will go and stretch our legs in the forest anyway. You're lucky – you've had your exercise for today!' she said with a grin. Arthur laughed, and went over to join the other pages.

Gwen and Flora waited until the boys went off to watch the squires compete, and then quickly slipped into the trees. Gwen led the way. She was used to being in the forest and knew how to find her way around. 'The Lake is south-west of here. We have to keep heading that way.'

Hearing a rustle behind them she glanced round uneasily, reaching instinctively to her shoulder where her bow usually sat and felt her heart sink. She would feel so much happier if she had it with her.

At long last, the two girls came through the

trees and saw the Lake shining in front of them, its still surface glittering like a sheet of silver. A purple mist hovered over the centre, hiding the island of Avalon. Gwen and Flora ran towards the black rocks at the edge of the water. Before they could say anything, light flashed and the waters parted. Nineve rose up from the Lake, her long chestnut hair falling to her bare feet. Her green and blue dress shimmered in the light.

'Guinevere! Flora!' the Lady of the Lake called, a smile lighting up her beautiful face. She floated across the surface of the Lake towards them and stopped by the rocks, taking care to keep her feet in the water.

Gwen knew Nineve couldn't leave the Lake as she had cast a spell to make it impossible for Morgana to cross the water to Avalon, but the enchantment would only work while Nineve herself was in the Lake. The spell would only last until the next lunar eclipse. If all eight Spell Sisters were not freed by then, Nineve wouldn't be able to stop Morgana from reaching Avalon and claiming it as her own.

Gwen stepped forward eagerly. 'Hello, Nineve! We came as quickly as we could. Can you show us where the next Spell Sister is trapped?' she asked.

In reply, Nineve held out one hand, palm up, and passed her other hand over it. Instantly, a pile of glittering silver dust appeared. She scattered it gently on the water between herself and the girls and blew gently. The girls watched, fascinated, as the dust started to form into shapes. At first, it was like a moving puzzle, and they couldn't quite make out the picture it was showing them. But then the movement slowed, and the girls saw an

image forming of an old round castle. It stood on top of a small hill, surrounded by a moat and a stone wall with a drawbridge set in it.

'This is what my magic has shown me,' Nineve told them. 'I believe it is where Amelia must be.'

'How do we find it?' asked Flora.

Nineve's eyes grew anxious. 'I do not know. All I can show you is this picture.'

Gwen frowned. There were so many castles nearby. 'It could be anywhere,' she said. Wracking her brain, she looked into Nineve's eyes. A memory stirred. . .

'Merlin!' she gasped. She saw a confused look cross Nineve's face.

'Who?' said Flora.

'That old man at the tournament. The peddler – only he wasn't just a peddler.' Gwen turned to Nineve. 'We met an old man with a long white beard at the tournament. He said his name was Merlin, and he seemed to know all about Avalon and even who I was.'

Nineve's eyes grew warm. 'Ah, yes,' she said softly. 'Merlin and I are very old friends, and he knows all about Avalon. I had no idea he was travelling around these parts again. What did he say to you? Did he tell you anything that might help? Think hard, Guinevere.'

'He. . . he told me a rhyme. He said it was part of my fortune.' Gwen spoke the rhyme out loud:

*'To a nearby castle you will go*
*And there confront your greatest foe*
*In a valley named for light*
*An evil darkness to put right.'*

'Do you think he was talking about the castle where Amelia is?' Flora exclaimed.

Nineve nodded. 'I am sure of it. He has given us the clue we need!'

'So we have to find a valley named for light.' Gwen's eyes widened as a thought came to her. 'I know! There's a village called Sunnyvale in a valley near to here. We passed it on our way to Clement Castle. The castle in the picture must be around there.'

'I think you're right,' Nineve said, smiling.

'Let's go!' said Flora eagerly.

Gwen lifted her hands to her mouth and

whistled loudly. There was the sound of hooves and a beautiful snow-white stallion came bursting through the trees.

'Moonlight!' smiled Gwen as the stallion halted in front of her and nuzzled her hands. He whinnied in delight.

Flora stroked his neck. 'It's so good to see you again, Moonlight.'

The girls had met Moonlight in the woods when they had set out on their first adventure. Gwen had fed him an apple from Avalon, which had given him magical powers. Ever since then, he had helped them as they tried to find the Spell Sisters. He lived wild in the forest, but he always came whenever they needed him. The magic of Avalon meant that he could gallop much faster than any normal horse!

Gwen climbed on to Moonlight's back and

then held out her hand to help Flora up behind her. 'We need to go to Sunnyvale village,' she told Moonlight.

'Travel quickly,' called Nineve. 'I do so hope you find Amelia.'

'We will!' Gwen declared. 'And we'll rescue her and bring her back.'

'Goodbye, Nineve!' Flora called.

'Goodbye!' Nineve raised her hand. 'May Avalon's magic keep you safe.'

Gwen touched her heels to Moonlight's sides and he cantered into the trees, but instead of speeding up, after a few strides he slowed and stopped. 'Walk on!' Gwen told him, but Moonlight shook his head and backed up.

'What is it, boy?' Gwen asked. Moonlight stamped his hoof uneasily.

'What's wrong with him?' asked Flora,

sounding worried.

'I don't know.' Gwen clicked her tongue. 'Come on, Moonlight!'

Just then, her sharp ears picked up a rustle in the bushes ahead. 'I think there's something out there that's upsetting him,' she said. She dismounted. 'I'll go and see what it is.'

'Be careful!' Flora said in alarm.

Now really wishing she had her bow and arrows, Gwen edged cautiously towards the noise. There it was again. A definite rustling of leaves. She could see the bramble bush ahead shaking as if there was something behind it. Was it a wild animal? Her heart beating fast, she crept up and looked quickly round the bush. 'Mark!' she gasped in surprise.

The little boy jumped. He'd had his back to the path and hadn't noticed her approaching.

'Gwen! What are you doing here?'

'I could ask you the same question,' Gwen said, putting her hands on her hips.

'I came to practise with these,' Mark said, holding something out.

'My bow and arrows!' exclaimed Gwen, immediately recognising her red-brown bow and battered leather quiver – a pouch filled with arrows tipped with white and red hen feathers.

'They're yours?' Mark said in surprise. 'I found them in the pavilion.' He blushed. 'I . . . I thought no one would mind if I borrowed them for a while. Everyone was watching the contest so I sneaked away with them. Please don't be cross with me!' Gwen saw his eyes fill with tears and she shook her head and smiled.

'It's all right. I'm not angry with you. I'm just glad my bow and arrows are safe.'

Mark handed them back to her and she slung the bow over her shoulder on a strap then tied the quiver around her waist. She felt much better having them with her. It was very lucky they'd come across the little boy in the woods. It occurred to Gwen suddenly that it might have been the reason Moonlight stopped. He wasn't scared – he was helping them!

'Will you take me home?' Mark asked. 'I think I'm lost.' As he spoke, he stood up and saw Flora and Moonlight over the top of the bramble bush. 'Look at that horse!' he exclaimed. 'He's amazing! Who does he belong to?'

Gwen's mind raced frantically. 'He's, um. . . He's sort of ours.'

'Yours?'

Gwen sighed. 'Yes.'

Mark hurried towards Flora and Moonlight. Gwen saw the alarm flash across Flora's face.

'Hello, Flora!' Mark called, waving. 'Gwen says this is your horse. Why doesn't he have a saddle and bridle on? And why is he out here in the forest?'

'Um. . . er. . .' Flora stammered.

The girls looked at each other helplessly. They couldn't tell Mark the truth. What were they going to do?

Gwen suddenly had an idea. 'Come to the Lake, Mark. I think you should meet a friend of ours.'

Flora leaned over. 'What are you doing?'

she whispered. 'We can't take him to Nineve.'

'Maybe she can cast a forgetting spell or something on him,' Gwen whispered back. 'He's lost. We can't leave him out here on his own, but we have to do something quickly. We need to get to Sunnyvale! Let's see what Nineve says.'

'What are you two whispering about?' asked Mark.

'Nothing,' Gwen replied hastily. 'Let's go.'

She quickly helped the little boy on to Moonlight's back – he was small enough that the stallion could carry all three of them. They galloped through the trees, and when they got to the Lake, Gwen called softly: 'Nineve!'

She had hardly finished saying her name before Nineve was rising up through the water. Mark squeaked in alarm, and as Nineve floated across the water towards them, he hid behind Gwen.

'Don't be afraid,' said Gwen, taking his hand.

Nineve reached them, and Gwen explained what had happened. 'Would you be able to cast a forgetting spell or something?' she finished. 'We don't want him to tell everyone in the castle about Moonlight – and about you, and—'

Nineve held up her hands. 'I could, but I don't think I need to use magic. I feel certain he can be trusted.' Nineve looked past Gwen. 'Mark, come here!' she called softly.

Mark swallowed and slowly walked round Gwen to the edge of the Lake, his eyes as large as dinner plates. He bowed before Nineve and stared at her in awe. 'You're the most beautiful lady I have ever seen!'

She smiled. 'Thank you. You speak like a

true knight.' Nineve crouched down so she was at eye level with him. 'Now, it is very important that no one knows about me or about Moonlight the stallion, or even that the girls were here. Great danger could come to the kingdom if people found out. Can I trust you? Will you keep all that you have seen here today a secret?'

Mark looked thrilled. 'Of course I will, my lady!' he vowed. 'I promise!'

Nineve looked deep into his eyes. He stared

back, his gaze open and honest. She smiled. 'Thank you, Mark. Go back with the girls now and remember: never tell anyone about what you have seen today.' She straightened up, her smile widening.

'We'll take him back so we know he's home safely, then we'll set out to find Amelia,' Gwen said.

'But what if he does tell someone?' said Flora anxiously.

'I won't!' Mark declared firmly. 'I won't ever put you or the kingdom in danger!'

Nineve nodded. 'He can be trusted.'

Gwen relaxed. If Nineve believed Mark, she knew she could trust him too. 'We'd better get going,' she said.

Calling goodbye to Nineve, they set off on Moonlight through the trees. Mark whooped as the stallion went faster and faster, the trees blurring around them as they wove through the forest. They reached the trees by Clement Castle in just a few minutes.

'That was amazing!' Mark gasped, his eyes glowing as Gwen helped him down. In the distance was the sound of the tournament still going on – the cheering and the clash of metal as the squires fought.

'Enjoy watching the rest of the contest!' Gwen said.

'Thank you for bringing me back.' Mark looked at her in admiration. 'I always thought it must be dull being a girl – but you have lots more fun than the boring pages do! Do all girls have wild horses and know magic ladies in lakes?'

Gwen hid her grin. 'Well, not quite all! Now go back to the others, and remember your promise to keep our secret.'

'I will,' said Mark. 'See you at supper!'

With a final wave, he hurried back to the castle through the trees.

'Phew!' Gwen said as she climbed back on to Moonlight. 'At least he's safe. But now we don't have much time. We'd better go and find Amelia!'

Flora nodded. 'Yes, let's go!'

Gwen clicked her tongue and leaned forwards. 'Come on, Moonlight!'

With a wild whinny, the stallion wheeled round and sped away.

# 6

## Sunnyvale Castle

Moonlight raced through the woods, his hooves sending up flurries of red and gold leaves. The girls clung to his back as he carried them to Sunnyvale, only stopping when they reached the top of the valley. Down below them, next to a sparkling river, was a small village with cottages and a few farms. Smoke wafted out of chimneys into the blue sky and cattle grazed on the land nearby. Gwen remembered it from when they had ridden past on their way to Clement Castle.

'There it is. That's Sunnyvale,' she said to Flora.

'And that must be the castle we're looking for!' exclaimed Flora, pointing to the far side of the valley. The castle was set on a small mound but was almost completely hidden by trees. It could only just be seen from where they were standing. They rode Moonlight down into the valley, steering clear of the village.

Moonlight splashed through the shallow stream at the bottom before cantering up the other side of the valley, passing a tumble-down farm with two stone barns. There was a discarded cartwheel on the ground and an old ladder leaning against one of the barn walls. A collie dog came running out, barking at them. The girls looked round anxiously, but there was no sign of anyone, and so Moonlight continued on his way.

Near the top of the sloping sides of the valley they reached the castle moat, which ran around the bottom of the small hill the castle was built on. But instead of water, it was filled with a dark sludgy mud. The only way across it was over the wooden drawbridge built into the gatehouse on the outer wall of the castle, but the bridge was pulled up, blocking the entrance to the castle.

'Hello?' called Gwen cautiously.

'Is anyone there?' echoed Flora.

Castles were normally hives of activity, with people coming and going, animals grazing, smoke coming from the fires and cooking smells from the kitchens. Even a small castle like this would usually have a gatekeeper in the gatehouse watching for visitors, but nobody came in response to their calls. 'It seems to be deserted,' Gwen said. 'But how can it be? There has to be someone in there to have pulled up the drawbridge.'

'Unless it was pulled up by magic,' Flora said slowly. They looked at each other.

'Morgana's probably used her powers to shut it, to stop anyone getting in,' said Gwen in dismay. 'How are we going to get it down? The lever to lower it will be inside the gatehouse. We have to somehow get across the moat and then get over the wall.'

'I'll never manage that,' said Flora sadly. Gwen knew Flora wasn't much for climbing or jumping. Her mind raced as she looked at the sludgy mud in the moat. It was hard to tell how deep it was, but even if it was shallow enough to wade through, she didn't fancy it. Still, they had to get inside – Amelia needed their help.

'If we could just get over the moat somehow then. . .' Gwen looked at the raised drawbridge. 'Maybe I could use my arrows to climb up and over the drawbridge and into the gatehouse, and then I could let the drawbridge down so you could come in.'

Flora stared at her. 'How?'

Gwen dismounted, lifted her bow and slipped an arrow from her quiver. 'Like this!' Resting the arrow against the bow, she eased the notch on to the bowstring. Then she raised the bow and pulled back the string, holding it tight. She stared down the arrow shaft and breathed out, letting the arrow go. It shot through the air, hitting the drawbridge exactly where she wanted. The shaft shook with the impact, but its point stuck firmly into the wood. Gwen followed it with another arrow slightly above it and to one side, and then another further up again.

Flora realised what she was doing. 'You're going to climb up the arrows!'

Gwen nodded and shot a column of arrows one above the other all the way up to the top of the drawbridge. Her aim was perfect. 'I *knew* I'd need my bow and arrows today!' she said with a smile. 'Now I've got a way of climbing up, but first we have to get over the moat.' She looked around. 'What

we need is a long plank of wood, or a ladder or something, which we can use as a bridge.'

'A ladder!' gasped Flora. 'There was one at that farm we passed, do you remember? Maybe we could borrow it.'

'Good plan!' Gwen vaulted back on to Moonlight in front of Flora and they galloped back to the farm. The collie dog was chasing a

cat, but no one came in answer to their calls.

'We'll just have to take it,' said Gwen, going over to the tall ladder and examining it.

'But what if someone needs it?' Flora asked anxiously.

'We'rejustborrowing

it. We'll bring it back,' said Gwen. 'I bet the whole household have gone to the tournament. Besides, what we're doing is important. Amelia needs us.' She frowned at the ladder. 'How do we get it back to the castle, though? It's really big and heavy.'

'We'll just have to carry it,' said Flora. 'You take one end and I'll take the other.'

'Are you sure?' Gwen asked doubtfully. She knew that Flora was even clumsier than usual when she had to lift or carry things.

Flora nodded determinedly. 'It's the only way.'

Without complaining, Flora took one end of the ladder and Gwen took the other and they started back up the hill with Moonlight walking alongside them. It was hard work, and Gwen was very glad Flora was there with her, even though her cousin tripped over twice on the way back to the castle! Still, it would have been impossible without the two of them.

'Almost there!' Gwen panted as they headed into the trees.

Reaching the moat, they stopped to get their breath back. Their hands were filthy and their faces smudged as they stood the ladder up on one end. Was it going to be long enough to reach all the way across? There was only one way to find out!

'One, two. . . three!' called Gwen, and they let the ladder fall. To the girls' relief, the top of it landed on the far side of the moat.

Flora looked at the ladder and then at the mud beneath it. 'It doesn't look very safe.'

'Why don't you wait here?' suggested Gwen. 'I'll go over it, climb the arrows and then hopefully

get into the gatehouse and let the drawbridge down. Then you could cross that.'

'No.' Flora shook her head. 'After all, what if you slip or need help when you're climbing up? I should come with you.'

'All right. I'll go first.' Gwen gave Moonlight a pat. 'We'll be back soon, boy. Wait here for us while we go to find Amelia.'

The horse nuzzled her and then wandered away to graze. Hitching up her skirts, Gwen crawled on to the ladder and began to move across on her hands and knees. The wood had some splinters in it, but she ignored the scratches and pricks. She could see the sludge below. She really didn't want to fall into it! With a relieved sigh, Gwen reached the other side and crawled off.

'Come on!' she called to Flora.

Flora swallowed. 'I wish I wasn't so clumsy.'

'Just be careful as you go,' Gwen said.

Hesitantly, Flora started to crawl across. 'I don't like this!' she said, looking down at the moat beneath and trembling.

'You can do it!' said Gwen encouragingly.

Flora edged forward again. She got closer and closer to Gwen, but just when she was almost at the other side, her shaking hands lost their grip and she slipped to one side. She rolled over the edge and the ladder tipped over!

'Flora!' Gwen cried as her cousin shrieked and fell into the moat.

*Splosh!* Flora hit the sludge.

Gwen started to scramble down the banks of the moat, hanging on to clumps of long grass so she didn't fall in herself. To her relief, Flora stood up. She wasn't hurt, and luckily the moat wasn't that deep so the sludge only came to her waist.

'Look at me!' Flora cried in dismay, looking down at her ruined dress and cloak.

Gwen's heart was still pounding. 'At least you're not hurt. Here, let me help you.' She reached out and Flora took her hand. Hanging on to the clumps of grass, Gwen helped her up the bank.

Flora flopped down, panting. 'Yuck!' she said, wiping her hands on the grass. Gwen handed her a handkerchief and Flora cleaned her face and neck with it, but her new dress was ruined. 'Whatever is Mother going to say when I go back to the tournament like this!' she groaned.

Gwen hugged her. 'We'll sort that out later. For now we need to get into that castle and rescue Amelia.' She stood up. 'I'm going to try and get into the gatehouse.'

'Be careful!' Flora said anxiously.

Gwen went to the drawbridge and looked up. She was good at climbing, but the drawbridge was high and she wasn't sure how stable the arrows were. She knew she didn't have a choice, though. They had to get inside, and quickly.

Ignoring the fear that was prickling at her scalp, she reached for the first arrow. It held firm.

*Here goes*, she thought to herself. *It's time to climb!*

# 7

# Freeing Amelia

Heart in her mouth, Gwen began to climb up the drawbridge using the arrows as hand- and footholds. She fixed her gaze on the top. If she could just climb over it, she could then get over the wall and should find herself on a walkway around the top of the castle. Gwen hoped she could get from there into the gatehouse. *Just keep going*, she told herself firmly.

She moved up one arrow and then the next until she was almost at the top. Reaching for the final arrow, she grabbed it with her right hand. A feeling of triumph surged through her, but then the arrow came out of the wood! Gwen gasped as she felt herself lurch backwards with the arrow still in her hand.

Flora shrieked from below, but luckily Gwen still had a firm grip on the arrow she was holding with her other hand. Steadying herself, Gwen took several deep breaths, clinging on hard. She knew she mustn't look down. Using all her strength, she reached up and pushed the loose arrow back into the hole it had come from. It wouldn't be a great support now, but if she moved quickly, she might be able to hold on to it long enough to pull herself up to the top of the wall.

'Be careful!' Flora shouted, her voice shaky with fright.

Gwen gathered all her courage and finished the climb. Her fingers clutched frantically at the top of the wall, and with a desperate wriggle, she swung herself over, falling into a heap on to the stone walkway on the other side.

For a moment Gwen lay there, unable to do anything but gasp, but gradually her heartbeat slowed and her breathing returned to normal. She'd done it! She was safe!

Gwen got to her feet and looked over the wall to wave down at Flora, who was still looking very worried. 'I'm all right!' she shouted to her cousin. 'And. . .' She looked around. 'I was right! I can get into the gatehouse from here!'

A small doorway led from the walkway into the gatehouse room. Gwen rushed in and spotted the handle that would lower the drawbridge. She turned it quickly, hoping it would work. The chains holding up the bridge began to rattle, and then the drawbridge started to lower!

As soon as it was down, Gwen ran down a stone spiral staircase to the bottom of the gatehouse, just in time to meet Flora as she ran into the castle.

'You did it!' Flora cried. She hugged Gwen.

'I'm just glad we're finally in. Now we have to hurry and rescue Amelia before sunset. We can't risk being late back to the castle and I don't fancy being here when it's dark,' said Gwen breathlessly.

Flora nodded quickly. 'Where do you think she's trapped?'

They both looked around the small courtyard. There were empty kitchens to the left, and a round tower with narrow slits for windows dotted across its walls. A lone raven was perched at the top of the tower. It gave a caw and flapped away into the sky.

Gwen spotted a wooden staircase leading up to a studded oak door. 'I think the main hall must be up those stairs,' she said. Most castles were built in much the same way, so she was willing to guess she was right. Gwen raced up the steps. Reaching the door, she turned the big iron handle and it creaked open. Sure enough, it led into an enormous hall.

There was a long oak table in the centre surrounded by chairs, an empty fireplace and a side table piled with dull silver plates, knives and goblets. Dusty tapestries hung on the walls, embroidered with pictures of battles, knights and armies. The candles in the holders on the walls had burned out long ago, and the only light came from the open door and the slit windows. Everywhere was still, apart from the specks of dust dancing in the sun's rays. Silence hung heavily in the air.

Gwen walked slowly around, taking it all in. The castle looked as though it had been suddenly abandoned. She didn't like the feel of the air in the room; it was as though something bad had happened there.

'This is creepy, Gwen. I don't like it,' Flora whispered.

'Me neither. But it's just the kind of place Morgana might have trapped Amelia, isn't it?'

Flora nodded. 'Let's find her quickly so we can get out of here.'

'She might be hidden somewhere unusual,' Gwen reminded her cousin. Morgana didn't just imprison the sisters – she usually disguised them too, which made it even harder for them to be freed. So far, they'd found one sister imprisoned in a tree, another hidden inside a metal gateway and the third trapped in a cave wall.

Gwen looked carefully around the room. She couldn't see anywhere that Amelia might be trapped. She spotted a stone staircase at the back of the hall that led to the second floor. 'Maybe she's upstairs?' she suggested.

'Gwen! Wait!' Gwen turned. Flora was standing by one of the faded tapestries. 'Come and see this.'

Gwen went over. The tapestry was dusty, but she saw that instead of the usual pictures of battles and knights, it was embroidered with dull

gold thread, and showed a picture of a frightened-looking girl with long blonde hair. Gwen was instantly reminded of the three sisters they had freed already. She caught her breath. 'It must be Amelia!'

'Set her free!' Flora urged. 'Quick, Gwen!'

Heart racing, Gwen pulled the pendant over her head and held it to the tapestry. Gwen began to chant the special spell Nineve had taught her:

*'Spell Sister of Avalon I—'*

Suddenly a violent wind swirled around the room, interrupting Gwen as it sent chairs crashing over and flung small objects into the walls. Flora and

Gwen were swept off their feet. Gwen cried out as she hit the stone floor. She gripped her pendant in one hand as the wind continued to batter her. Lifting her head, she saw her cousin lying nearby. 'Flora! Are you all right?' she shouted.

Her words were almost whipped away by the whistling wind, but Flora caught what she was saying. 'Yes!' she shouted back, her plaits whirling around her. Flora's eyes suddenly widened and she pointed behind Gwen.

Gwen looked round and saw the wind ripping Amelia's tapestry away from the wall. The two bottom corners had already come loose. The tapestry flapped wildly for a moment, before the top corners tore away from the nails holding them in place.

The tapestry flew past Gwen and towards the enormous fireplace. It was going to go up the chimney! Just in time, Gwen leaped through the air and caught hold of a corner.

The wind tore at the tapestry furiously as though it had a mind of its own, but Gwen refused to let go. She pulled it to the ground and thrust her blue pendant against the woven fabric. She panted the magical phrase above the wind:

*'Spell Sister of Avalon I now release,*
*Return to the island and help bring peace!'*

What would happen? Gwen held her breath as a flash of gold raced across the surface of the tapestry. The threads began to unravel in front of her eyes, separating into sparkling strands of gold. They swirled into the air, and in spite of the roaring wind, before Gwen's eyes they formed into the shape of a beautiful young woman.

A shiver ran through the figure and suddenly she was standing there, solid and real, her blonde hair swirling to her feet, her eyes wide with relief.

The wind suddenly stopped, and there was a moment of complete silence. It was broken by the girl, who stepped towards Gwen with a smile. 'Thank you so much! You rescued me!'

'Amelia?' said Gwen.

'Yes, I am Amelia, one of the Spell Sisters of Avalon.' Amelia was wearing a purple dress trimmed with silver. Her long hair was secured by a silver headband decorated with tiny lilac gems; she had a very determined mouth and deep violet-blue eyes. 'Who are you?'

'I'm Gwen, and this is my cousin Flora,' Gwen replied as Flora rushed over to join her. 'Nineve sent us to rescue you.'

'We know what your sister, Morgana, is

trying to do,' added Flora. 'We've rescued three of your other sisters so far – Lily, Sophia and Isabella.'

'Thank goodness they are safe!' Amelia exclaimed. 'And thank you for freeing me.' She looked around as if she couldn't quite believe it. 'I thought I was going to be trapped here forever.'

'You must get back to Avalon,' Gwen said quickly.

'Absolutely,' said Amelia, nodding. 'Morgana could come back at any second. Shall we go?'

They all nodded and ran towards the heavy door. Gwen heaved it open. As she did so, a dark shape with a razor-sharp beak flew straight at her face.

Gwen yelled in surprise and ducked. The raven swooped up with a harsh caw that sounded almost like laughter. Then instantly, the air was filled with the sounds of more ravens cawing and shrieking. Gwen stopped dead. There were now hundreds of the large black birds perched on the top of the outer wall of the castle and around the gatehouse. They were all staring at Gwen, Flora and Amelia, their eyes gleaming darkly above their sharp beaks.

'What's happening?' gasped Flora. 'Where have they all come from!'

There wasn't a shred of doubt in Gwen's mind.

'Morgana!' she gasped.

# 8

# The Eye of the Storm

Gwen reached for her bow, but as she did so, all of the ravens' cawing voices came together as one. *'You shall not escape!'* they shrieked in a single voice. *'I shall not let you get away this time!'*

'It is Morgana!' exclaimed Gwen. 'She's speaking through the birds.'

'She must have created that awful

wind too,' Flora whispered.

The ravens opened their mouths together. *'Did you think I would let you escape so easily?'* They screeched. *'You will not return to Avalon. It shall be mine!'*

'No!' Gwen protested.

'You're not having Avalon, Morgana!' Amelia declared furiously. Her words were drowned by a huge thunderclap.

*'You will not escape!'* The ravens still cawed Morgana's words. *'I will make sure of it!'*

Flora grabbed Gwen's arm.

Flying up into the air, the ravens raced away as dark storm clouds swept with incredible speed across the sky. Lightning flashed out from the clouds, zigzagging down and hitting the ground just in front of where the girls and Amelia were standing. They all screamed and jumped back.

There was another crash of thunder and another bolt of lightning. If they didn't move fast, they were going to be hit!

'Quick!' Amelia pulled Flora back inside the hall and Gwen slammed the door shut behind them. Outside they could hear the thunder crashing and see the flashes of lightning through the slit windows. It was very dim in the hall with the door shut. Gwen stood in the gloom, her heart racing.

'What are we going to do?' Flora's voice quavered.

'We can't go back out there. We'll get hit by lightning!' said Amelia.

'Oh, no! What about Moonlight?' said Flora suddenly.

'Who's Moonlight?' asked Amelia in alarm.

'Our horse. He'll be all right,' said Gwen

quickly, looking at Flora. 'I bet he'll just gallop away into the woods and get away from the storm. He's clever enough to know he should find shelter. But what are we going to do?'

'We have to escape somehow!' Amelia's face creased into a frown. 'Morgana cannot get away with this.'

'But what can we do?' said Flora.

Amelia looked thoughtful. 'Well, she's not going to be able to keep this storm going forever. Conjuring thunder and lightning takes a lot of power. Morgana is strong, but even she cannot keep a storm going for too long. I think we should just wait until she tires, and then try and escape while she's recovering.'

Gwen nodded.

'It's dark in here, though,' said Flora unhappily. 'I don't like it.'

'We'll be all right,' said Amelia, taking the girls' hands.

'And at least we're safe with the door shut,' added Gwen.

But as the words left her mouth, there was a rushing, howling sound and a whirlwind swept down the chimney and out into the room! It was ten times as strong as the previous wind. Swirling like a typhoon it tore the remaining heavy tapestries off the walls as easily as if they were pieces of paper, and sent the massive table crashing over on its side, sweeping it towards the wall. Flora, Gwen and Amelia were all lifted off their feet and flung into the air.

'Hang on to each other!' cried Gwen, but it was no use. The wind was too strong. Their hands were wrenched apart and they were swept through the air like rag dolls. Gwen felt herself

tumbling over and over and then she banged into a wall. She collapsed in a heap and saw to her relief that the big table was nearby. It was on its side, its legs wedged against the wall. She managed to grab one of the legs and pull herself behind it. The tabletop acted as a shield, keeping her from the worst of the fierce wind, but plates, goblets and knives were flying precariously close by.

Gwen could see Flora nearby also pressed

against the wall by the force of the wind. Hanging on to one table leg for support, Gwen reached out and grabbed Flora's arm and hung on for dear life. 'Try and get behind here!' she shouted to her cousin.

With Gwen's help, Flora managed to scramble behind the table too. They ducked down for cover. 'Thanks!' she panted. 'But where's Amelia?'

They both looked over the edge anxiously,

squinting against the howling wind. Amelia was being swept across the floor. She tried to grab on to a chair to stop herself, but it was no use.

'Amelia – duck!' Gwen yelled at the top of her voice as she saw a silver plate heading straight for Amelia's head.

Amelia bobbed her head down and the plate flew past her. She let go of the chair and was swept towards the table, but was just too far away for Gwen to reach out and grab her.

Her mind racing, Gwen pulled off the long silken belt from her dress. 'Amelia! Catch this!' She flung out the end of the belt so it fell just in front of Amelia, who grabbed it and hung on tight. Gwen held on to the other end with all her might, and was almost pulled out from behind the table by Amelia's weight, but Flora grabbed her round the waist. 'Hang on to her, Gwen!' she cried.

Together they pulled and pulled, helping Amelia fight against the wind and get behind the tabletop with them.

'Oh, thank you!' Amelia gasped.

They all crouched down behind the table.

It was hard to hear each other above the wind and the sound of the objects crashing into the walls.

'What do we now?' said Gwen, her heart pounding.

'Will Morgana find it hard to keep this wind going?' Flora asked Amelia.

Amelia shook her head. 'It takes a lot of power to create a storm outside, but not much to keep a wind like this swirling through a single room. Morgana could keep this wind going for days.'

'*Days?*' Gwen exclaimed as a chair crashed into the tabletop, making it shake.

Amelia nodded, her brow knitted with concern. 'And while she has us trapped here, it gives her a chance to think of what else she could do to us.'

'Then we have to get out as quickly as possible,' said Gwen. She jumped as a goblet smashed into the wall above her. 'But how can we get to the door without being hurt?'

'Or worse!' said Flora as a knife followed the goblet.

'Maybe my magic can help,' said Amelia suddenly. 'Now you've freed me, my power has returned – I can make metals and minerals do as I will. I can stop the plates, knives and goblets flying around anyway. That should make it easier to get to the door.' She took a breath and shut her eyes, holding her hands out, palms up, beside her. Then she spoke softly:

*'Metals and minerals here in this hall*
*Come to me gently, obey my call.'*

A plate flew through the air and landed beside her. More plates followed, knives and goblets too. Amelia's power over them was strong, and despite the typhoon, the objects floated towards her, settling themselves down beside her in a huge pile. The wind still raged, but at least dangerous missiles were no longer flying around.

'That was a brilliant idea!' Flora said to Amelia.

Amelia smiled. 'Now we just need to find a way of reaching the door and getting out.'

Gwen peered over the tabletop at the door. Even without the metal cutlery flying around, there was still a whirlwind of other objects in the room. How could they possibly get past them?

'If there was something along the wall that we could cling on to, then we could try and stop ourselves being swept away while we make our way to the other side of the room,' said Flora.

Gwen looked around, but the curtains and tapestries and anything else they could have held on to had all been blown off the walls by Morgana's whirlwind. Then her eyes fell on the pile of silver objects beside Amelia. 'Hang on! What if Amelia makes a rod?'

Amelia looked puzzled. 'How can I do that?'

'Your magic!' Gwen exclaimed. She pointed to the pile of plates and other objects beside her. 'Do you think you could use these silver things, and cast a spell to mould them into something long enough to reach between here and the door?'

'I can at least try,' Amelia said, her eyes brightening hopefully. She looked at the pile of objects and then at the door and the floor and walls around her. There was an iron candleholder still fastened on to the wall just above their heads, and another on the other side of the room. 'I'll use the candleholders to anchor the rod on either side,' Amelia said, pointing at them. She settled down on her knees again, thought for a moment and then chanted another spell:

*'Plates and goblets here on this floor*
*Forge me a rod from candle to door.'*

She waved her hands above the pile of silver objects. They rose upwards and started to swirl together. Flora and Gwen watched in awe. Faster and faster the objects went until they were just a spinning cloud of silver, and then suddenly Amelia clapped her hands. There was a bright flash of light and the objects transformed into a long silver rod. It shot across the room like an arrow from a bow, hitting the metal handle on the

door and merging with it. At the same time, the other end attached itself to the iron candleholder on the wall.

'It worked!' said Amelia in triumph. There was now a solid rod fixed from the candleholder to the door just like a metal railing.

'Come on!' Gwen ducked out from behind the table. Instantly, the wind hit her, banging into her body with the force of a carthorse, but she stretched up, grabbed the rail with both hands and started to pull herself along. She had to half-shut her eyes, the wind was so strong. It tore through her hair and knocked her about, but gritting her teeth, Gwen held on to the rail and forced herself to inch towards the door.

Looking round, she saw that Flora and Amelia were following. The main door was getting closer and closer. Their hands grasped for the handle, and working together, they managed to turn it. The door swung open, and finally they could run outside!

'The storm outside has stopped!' Flora said as they looked around the courtyard. The last of the black clouds were disappearing towards the horizon. The sun was shining down and the sky was blue.

'Morgana must have tired herself out!' said Amelia. 'Hopefully we can escape now before she regains her strength.'

'Quick!' Gwen grabbed their hands and the three of them ran across the courtyard and over the drawbridge. As soon as they were on the other side, Amelia turned and called out a few words. Instantly, the chain that lifted and lowered the drawbridge started to move as if someone was turning the handle, and it shut tight against the wall. Amelia breathed a sigh of relief. 'Now no one else will be able to get in there while that awful wind still rages inside.'

'And we can get you back to Avalon!' said Gwen. She whistled. There was an answering whinny and Moonlight cantered out of the trees. He looked fine, untouched by lightning, wind or rain.

Gwen ran over and hugged him. 'Moonlight. Thank goodness you're all right!' She turned to Amelia. 'He'll take us back to the Lake. He can gallop really fast, thanks to Avalon's magic. Can you use your magic to get there?'

'Of course,' said Amelia. 'Thank you so much for all your help, girls.'

Gwen looked over at the moat and remembered something else. 'I don't suppose you could use your magic to transport another thing first?' she asked.

'Of course,' Amelia replied. 'What is it?'

Gwen pointed at the ladder the girls had borrowed from the farmyard. 'We have to return that to the farm nearby. Do you think you'd be able to?'

'With pleasure,' Amelia said with a grin. In the blink of an eye, the ladder had vanished! The girls thanked her gratefully.

'Now,' she said, 'I should be going too. I'll see you back at the Lake.' She clapped her hands, spun round and vanished in a flash of light.

Gwen vaulted up on to Moonlight and offered Flora her hand. Flora took it and scrambled up behind her.

'Let's get back to the Lake, Moonlight!' Gwen cried, and they galloped off.

# 9

# Amelia's gift

Nineve and Amelia were waiting for the girls when they arrived on Moonlight. Nineve hugged the girls and then cast the spell that allowed them all to walk across the surface of the still water of the Lake to Avalon. Gwen and Flora ran happily through the purple mist towards the island.

Gwen looked around, breathless. When she

had first found the pendant, Nineve had shown her a vision of what Avalon used to look like – a green island with sparkling streams, bright flowers, butterflies and bees flying through the air and hundreds of apple trees, with red and green apples hanging heavily on their branches. The Spell Sisters' house, set up a little path from the shore, had been bright and cheerful with smoke coming from its chimney. However, when Morgana had captured the sisters and taken their magic powers away, the island had started to die and the deserted house had become cold and dark.

Thankfully, since she and Flora had started rescuing the sisters there were new signs of life. The apple trees had tiny green buds on them, and the grass was starting to grow again. The butterflies and bees had returned, and smoke was coming from the chimney of the house once more. As the girls approached, the door flew open and Sophia, Lily and Isabella – the three sisters whom Gwen and Flora had already rescued – crowded the doorway.

'Amelia!' they cried.

'I'm home!' Amelia raced up the path to meet them. Her sisters met her with open arms.

Amelia looked round at Gwen and Flora, her blue eyes shining. 'Thank you so much for freeing me and helping me to get back to Avalon!' she held out her arms and the next moment, Gwen and Flora were joining in with the hugs.

'We can't thank you enough,' Sophia told them.

'It's so wonderful to have Amelia back,' added Lily.

'Come inside,' said Isabella, pulling them

both into the house.

A cheerful fire was burning in the fireplace, and the table was now laid with sparkling golden plates and goblets. 'We shall cook you a feast!' said Sophia. 'And you can tell us all about your adventures.'

'We'd love to stay,' said Gwen, squeezing her hand. 'But we really have to get back.'

'We're supposed to be watching a tournament,' Flora explained. 'If we're not back at the castle by suppertime, we'll get into trouble.'

'We understand,' said Lily. 'But thank you again for rescuing Amelia.'

'I would like to say thank you in my own way,' said Amelia, stepping forward. She gently touched Gwen's necklace where the blue pendant sat side by side with three gemstones, all of which had been given to Gwen by each of the sisters when she had returned them to Avalon. 'I shall add my own gemstone.'

She clasped her hands together and, lifting them to her lips, she whispered a word. When she opened her hands, Gwen and Flora saw a sparkling purple stone sitting there.

'Amethyst,' said Amelia softly. 'For courage and strength. It will bring help when you need it.' She blew softly on it. The stone rose in the air and floated towards the necklace. As it touched the silver chain there was a flash of purple light.

Gwen blinked, and in a split second, the stone had attached itself to the chain! Touching it with her fingers, she felt the tingle of magic.

'Thank you,' she said to Amelia. Then she looked at the other sisters, remembering the adventures she and Flora had been on so far. She grinned. 'We'll be back very soon.'

'When we rescue another of your sisters,' added Flora.

'We *will* stop Morgana before the lunar

eclipse, we promise,' Gwen finished.

Sophia smiled. 'If anyone can, it is you two.'

Gwen went to the door with Flora and they called goodbye.

'Goodbye!' the sisters all chorused. Then Gwen and Flora ran back down the path to where Nineve was waiting.

'You should be very proud of yourselves,' Nineve told the girls warmly when they reached the other side of the Lake. Moonlight was still there waiting for them, ready to take them back to Clement Castle. 'You were incredibly brave and so clever. It must have been terrifying trying to escape Morgana's spell.'

'It was,' Gwen admitted. 'But we got out, and we rescued Amelia. That's the important thing.'

'Next time may be just as difficult, if not more so.' The worry in Nineve's eyes deepened.

'Morgana will be furious that you have escaped, and with only four sisters still trapped, she will be more determined than ever.'

'She can't stop us,' said Gwen determinedly, looking at Flora, who nodded.

'We'll do everything we can,' Flora added.

Nineve smiled. 'I will be in touch as soon as I have found out where the next Spell Sister is. Travel safely. And. . .' A happy look lit up her eyes. 'If you happen to see Merlin again, please be sure to wish him my best.'

'We will,' said Gwen. They mounted Moonlight, Gwen clicked her tongue to him and calling their goodbyes, the girls set off through the trees.

✦ ✦ ✦

Moonlight galloped swiftly back to the castle. He stopped just by the edge of the treeline, and

Gwen and Flora dismounted quickly. The sun was already starting to set. 'Look after yourself, boy,' said Gwen. 'We'll call you again as soon as we need you.' The stallion nuzzled first her and then Flora before turning, tossing his head and trotting happily back into the forest.

Flora looked down at her dress. 'Look at me! Mother is going to be furious!' Her new blue dress was filthy from the moat and torn from when she had been thrown across the floor by the wind. 'I can't even try to wash and mend it. It's ruined – and Mother's expecting me to wear it tonight. What am I going to do?'

Gwen bit her lip – her dress was in an awful state too. It seemed so unfair that after having such an amazing adventure and rescuing another Spell Sister they were now going to get into trouble, but Flora was right. Aunt Matilda would be absolutely furious when she saw their clothes. 'I guess we just have to say sorry and put up with being punished.'

'Will you permit me to help?' said a soft voice. They swung round to see Merlin standing behind them in the shadows, leaning on a wooden staff. The hood of his dark green cloak was pulled up over his head, but there was no mistaking his lined face, bright blue eyes and long white beard.

'Merlin!' exclaimed Gwen. 'You wouldn't believe the adventure we've just had. Thank you so much – your fortune was exactly what we needed.'

A smile flickered across Merlin's face. 'I'm glad I could be of assistance.'

'Oh, and Nineve told us to wish you her best too!' Gwen said.

'Please pass my good wishes back. The Lady of the Lake and I are old friends. And you, I hope, will be my new friends. Will you permit me to help with your dresses?'

'But how?' Flora asked, raising her eyebrows in surprise.

Merlin smiled mysteriously. 'Close your eyes.' Gwen and Flora exchanged looks and then did as he asked. They heard Merlin mutter a word and felt a thump as he banged his staff against the earth. 'Open your eyes.'

The girls stared. Their dresses and cloaks were completely clean and mended. 'Oh my goodness!' gasped Gwen, picking up the folds of her dress and running her hands over her now clean cloak. She glanced back at Merlin only to realise he was no longer there. 'Flora, he's gone!'

Flora looked around wildly, but Merlin was nowhere to be seen. He had simply vanished. 'He really *is* magic!'

Gwen looked into the shadows of a nearby grove of trees. Was it her imagination or did something there move slightly? 'Thank you,' she whispered softly in case Merlin could still hear them. 'I hope we meet again.'

Flora took her hand. 'Let's get back to the castle.'

The squires' tournament had just ended and people were heading up to the castle for the feast. Gwen and Flora spotted Arthur, Will, Gawain and some of the other pages by Sir Richard's pavilion. Little Mark was with them, and when he spotted the girls, he came running over, with Arthur and Gawain close behind him.

'Hello there!' Mark said.

The girls waved, and Flora blushed as Gawain smiled broadly at her.

'Hello, Mark,' Gwen said. 'Have you been good?' She raised an eyebrow, and Mark nodded quickly.

'Mark told us about taking Gwen's arrows, and how you ladies found him when he was lost in the forest and brought him back,' Gawain said.

'Did he?' Gwen said, looking closely at Mark. Had the little boy kept their secret?

'Yes, I did. Thank you so much for bringing me back,' Mark said with a smile.

'Yes,' Gawain continued. 'It was very kind of you both.' He ruffled Mark's hair. 'Hopefully that will teach you a lesson about taking other

people's things and wandering off, Mark.'

'Oh yes, I won't do it again,' Mark said, looking at Gwen and Flora. 'After all, I might get into all sorts of adventures!'

Gwen and Flora hid their grins. So he had kept his word after all!

'So what were you doing in the forest? You missed the squires' contest,' Arthur said to Gwen as they all went over to the others.

'I know, but we just felt like stretching our legs,' replied Gwen.

Will had overheard and he sneered. 'I bet they went off to talk about dresses and embroidery and how to do their hair.' His feather bobbed on his new hat.

Gwen slipped her bow off her shoulder and took an arrow out of her quiver. 'Hmm, maybe we did,' she said lightly. 'Or maybe we were having exciting adventures – fighting evil, doing good, seeing magic happen.'

Will spluttered in her face. 'As if that's likely! Girls don't have adventures. You'd be useless at fighting evil! You can't even shoot a bow and arrow properly.'

'Can't I?' Gwen leaped forward and grabbed his hat.

'Hey! What are you doing?' Will yelled, trying to snatch it back. Gwen threw the hat high into the air. Lifting her bow and arrow up, she released the arrow in one swift movement. It pierced the hat and pinned it to a nearby tree, its long feather waving in the breeze.

Will roared. 'That's my new hat!'

Gwen looked at him innocently as the other pages fell about laughing. 'Oh, dear. What a pity. My arrow just kind of slipped.'

'You did it on purpose!' Will shouted furiously.

'Me? But how could I have?' Gwen said. 'After all, girls can't shoot, can they, Will?' She smiled sweetly at him. 'I'm sure you can easily climb up and get it, though, being a boy and all!' She took Flora's arm. Flora looked slightly shocked, but she was smiling too. 'Come on,

Flora, we should leave the boys to have their adventures,' Gwen said. 'Let's go and get ready for the feast!'

Giggling together, the two girls ran up the hill to the castle.

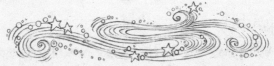

# In a Forest Clearing

The sun was setting in the sky, casting dark shadows across the forest floor.

'No!' shrieked Morgana Le Fay, emerging from her lair in the hollowed-out trunk of a huge oak tree.

Her raven was perched on her shoulder and she was holding her black twisted crown with dark jewels in her hands. Gradually the metal began to untwist and turn gold again, the jewels changing back to glowing rubies and emeralds.

Morgana threw it away with an enraged cry. It hit a tree trunk and landed in a pile of leaves. The raven flew up to a branch as Morgana stormed around the clearing like an angry bear.

'It has happened again! Those interfering girls have freed another of my sisters! Well, I will *not* lose any more of my powers. They will not triumph again! Avalon shall be mine and mine alone!'

She held out her arm and the raven flew down to land on it. 'Those girls have been lucky so far, but their luck has almost run out,' Morgana snarled. 'Next time they will not escape me!'

She swept back inside, the golden crown lying among the leaves, glittering in the last rays of the setting sun.

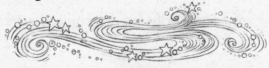